For my daughter April,
and son Daniel

First published in 1990
Copyright © Louise Maxwell, 1990
All rights reserved

Printed in Italy
for J.M. Dent & Sons Ltd
91 Clapham High Street
London SW4 7TA

British Library Cataloguing in Publication Data
Maxwell, Louise
The thorn in the lion's paw.
I. Title
823′.914 [F]
ISBN 0-460-88014-4

Illustrations for this book were prepared using acrylic
paints, pen and ink and pencil.

THE THORN IN THE LION'S PAW

Louise Maxwell

J.M. Dent & Sons Ltd
London

One night I heard something scratching
outside my door.

It was a lion

with a thorn in its paw.

I invited him in

and examined his foot.

When I touched the part that hurt,

he pulled away.

"Maybe some milk would calm my nerves
a little," said the lion.

We went to the larder.

The lion lapped up some milk,

and everything else he could see.

Soon all the shelves were bare,

but his nerves were no calmer.

Back in my room,
I tried to touch the paw again

but the lion jumped.
"Roarrr!"

The lion woke my mother,
who heard us and came to my room.

"What's going on in here?" she asked.

"It's a lion with a thorn in its paw," I answered.

"I see," she said, and she went back to bed.

Then I had a good idea.

I tied one part of my new school scarf
around the lion's neck,

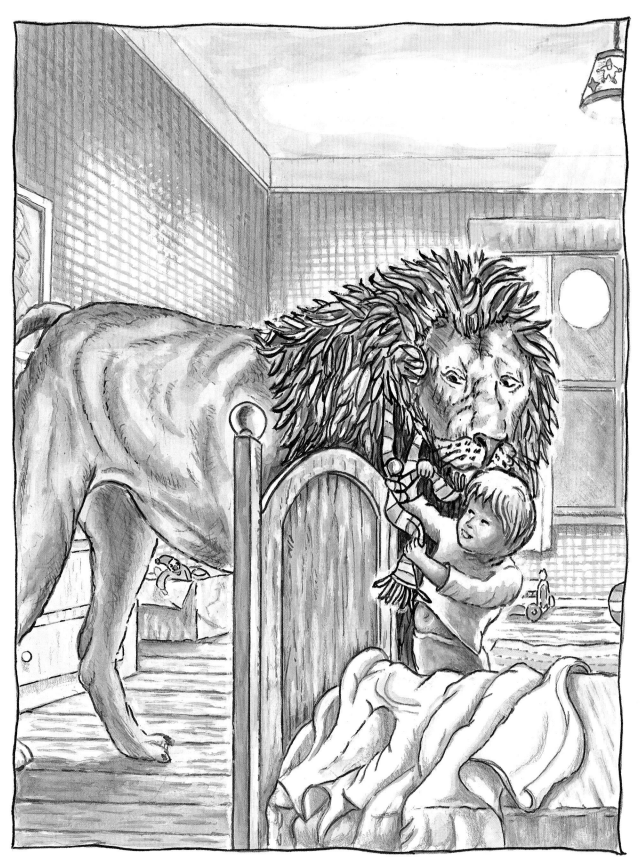

and tied the other parts around the bedpost.

The lion stretched out his injured foot.

I squeezed his paw.

The thorn popped out!

The lion was so pleased that
he gave me the thorn

to show to my friends at school.

...So I did.